This Book is a Gift of:
FRIENDS OF THE
LAFAYETTE LIBRARY
Contra Costa County Library

Virginia WOLF

Kyo Maclear

Isabelle Arsenault

Kids Can Press

One day my sister Virginia
woke up feeling wolfish.
She made wolf sounds
and did strange things...

When I painted her picture,
she growled,

"VANESSA... DOOOONNN'T."

When her friends rang the doorbell, she moaned,

"I'M NOT HOME."

She scared everyone away.

She said, "DO NOT WEAR THAT CHEERFUL YELLOW DRESS."

(My favorite dress!)

"DO NOT BRUSH YOUR TEETH SO LOUDLY."

She even told the bird to

"STOP THAT RACKET!"

She was a very bossy wolf.

The whole house sank.
Up became down.
Bright became dim.
Glad became gloom.

I did my best to cheer her up.
I offered her treats. She wolfed them all down.
But it made no difference. Nothing pleased her.
Not the cat. Not my violin. Not even
making faces at our brother Thoby.
She pulled up her covers and said,

"LEAVE ME ALONE."

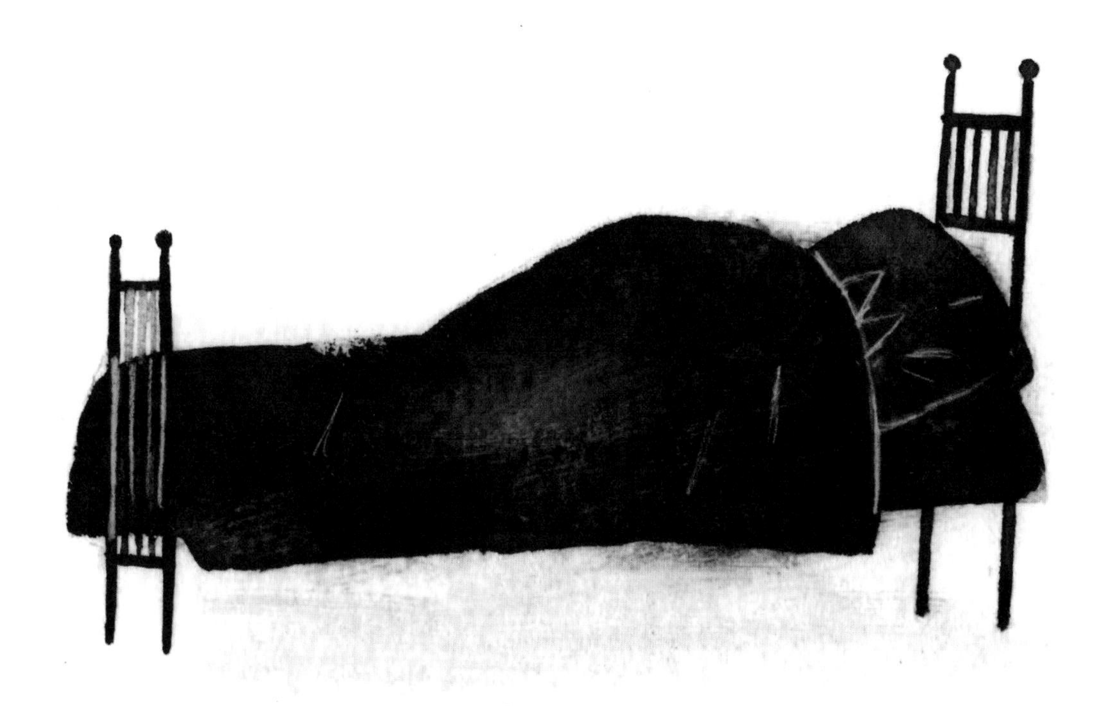

Then she said nothing.
To anybody.

I lay beside her on the bed.
We were two quiet lumps under the blanket.
We sank deep among the pillows.

We looked out the window and gazed at the sky.
We watched the clouds: a smudgy sailboat,
a flying llama and a floating castle.
It was like a whole other world.

Still, my sister said nothing. To anybody.

After a while, I said, "There must be something that will make everything feel better."

I said, "Please, Virginia."

I said, "Say something."

Finally she replied,

"IF I WERE FLYING RIGHT NOW I MIGHT FEEL BETTER."

"If you were flying, where would you like to go?"

I opened her atlas and named a few places.

"Paris. Tokyo. Mexico City—"

"NO. NO. NO!" she said.

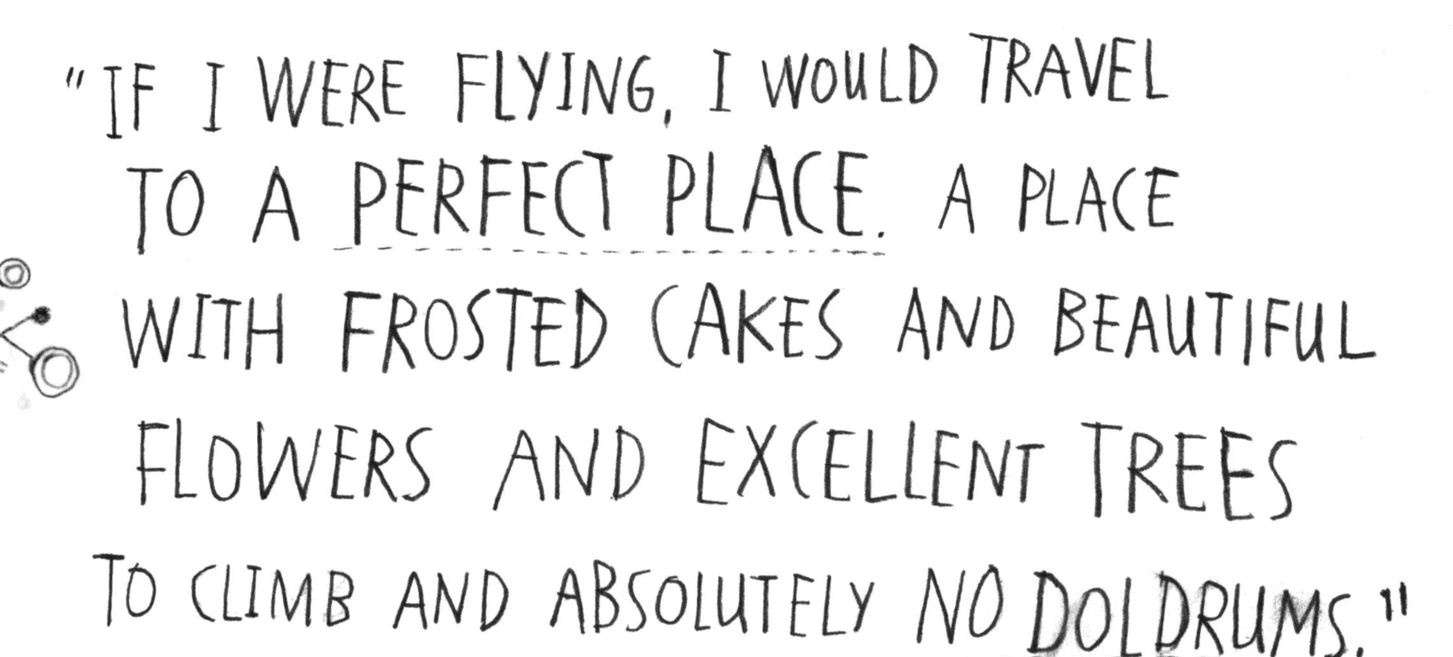

"IF I WERE FLYING, I WOULD TRAVEL TO A PERFECT PLACE. A PLACE WITH FROSTED CAKES AND BEAUTIFUL FLOWERS AND EXCELLENT TREES TO CLIMB AND ABSOLUTELY NO DOLDRUMS."

"Where is that?" I asked.

She thought for a moment and said, "BLOOMSBERRY, OF COURSE."

"Bloomsberry? Never heard of it. Is that near Burlington?"

She shook her head and sighed. "Buffalo?" I said.

"I DON'T THINK SO,"

she growled, slipping under the covers.

I flipped through her atlas but found no Bloomsberry.
No perfect place.
I didn't tell my sister.
But I had an idea.

I found my art box and a stack of paper and tiptoed around the room while my sister napped.

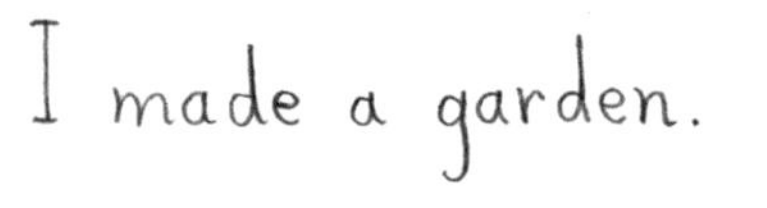

I made a garden.
I painted trees and strange candy blossoms and green shoots and frosted cakes. I painted leaves that said *hush* in the wind and fruit that squeaked, and slowly I created a place called Bloomsberry.
I made it look just the way it sounded.

My sister woke up.
At first she was too busy howling at the moon to notice what I was doing.

I painted a swing and a ladder that reached up to the window, so that what was down could climb up. My sister started to pay attention.

I brought the outside inside. I painted floating petals that looked like confetti. My sister stood up and helped. She said wolves like to wander around, so we painted a field with a big roaming space.

We made turquoise birds and
purple butterflies out of colored paper.
And Virginia told a story about a gray-shelled
snail that passed along the earth and
reached the top of a mountain
without realizing it.

The whole house lifted.
Down became up.
Dim became bright.
Gloom became glad.

When we were done,
it was past midnight.
Everyone slept soundly.

The next morning, my sister woke up and said,

"THE FLOWERS ARE FLOPPY." I nodded.

"THE TREES LOOK LIKE LOLLIPOPS." I nodded again.

"THAT SHRUB LOOKS LIKE AN ELEPHANT," she laughed.

"You hate it," I groaned.

"NO," she said. "IT'S PERFECT. I LOVE IT."

I smiled.

She looked different, so I asked her how she felt.
"MUCH BETTER," she said, looking a bit sheepish.
"Do you really feel better?" I asked.

"YES." She smiled and took my hand.
"NOW LET'S GO OUT AND PLAY."

To my sisters
(Nancy, Naomi, Kelly and Eliza)
and to the ever-lovely Bloomsberry group
(Isabelle, Tara and Karen P.).
With love and thankfulness — K.M.

To my dear and talented friend Vanessa A.,
as precious as a sister to me — I.A.

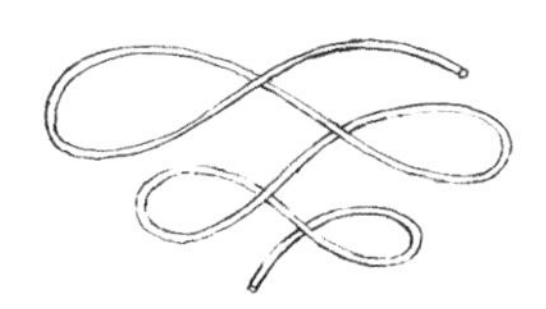

Kids Can Press acknowledges the financial support of the Government of Ontario, through the Ontario Media Development Corporation's Ontario Book Initiative; the Ontario Arts Council; the Canada Council for the Arts; and the Government of Canada, through the CBF, for our publishing activity.

Published in Canada by
Kids Can Press Ltd.
25 Dockside Drive
Toronto, ON M5A 0B5

Published in the U.S. by
Kids Can Press Ltd.
2250 Military Road
Tonawanda, NY 14150

www.kidscanpress.com

The artwork in this book was rendered in mixed media (ink, pencil, watercolor and gouache) and assembled digitally. The text was hand lettered by Isabelle Arsenault.

Edited by Tara Walker
Designed by Karen Powers

This book is smyth sewn casebound.
Manufactured in Tseung Kwan O, NT Hong Kong, China, in 04/2013 by Paramount Printing Co. Ltd.

CM 12 0 9 8 7 6 5 4

Library and Archives Canada Cataloguing in Publication

Maclear, Kyo, 1970–
Virginia Wolf / written by Kyo Maclear ; illustrated by Isabelle Arsenault.

ISBN 978-1-55453-649-8

I. Arsenault, Isabelle, 1978– II. Title.

PS8625.L435V57 2012 jC813'.6 C2011-904472-2

Kids Can Press is a Corus™ Entertainment company